Hit It!

Michael Hardcastle
Illustrated by Bob Moulder

A & C Black • London

Chapter One

Leaning left and then right, sharply twisting right again and then left, Scott cut into the penalty area. As he evaded one opponent after another the ball remained completely under his control.

He was sure he was going to score the goal that would lift the Aces up the league.

The Drilby goalkeeper was dithering.

The goalie had to decide whether to come out to narrow the angle for the shot.

Scott slowed down. He tried to pick his spot.

7

YES!

Kel was Scott's strike partner.

Scott caught up before they reached the centre circle.

What *do* you think you were doing?

That was my goal! I worked for it, I set it up.

But I scored it.

9

Kel grinned before charging forward after the ball. Scott and Kel had never been best friends off pitch but usually they weren't such deadly rivals on it.

Scott remained angry for the rest of the match and that didn't do his play any good. He missed an easy chance to side-foot the ball into the net so it was just as well that the Aces didn't concede a goal. They won 2-1 to move nearer the top of the league.

11

You were too slow. If Kel hadn't moved fast it could've been the opposition that took the ball off you. That red-haired defender was coming in at you but you weren't aware of him.
Good job Kel got there first.

Scott knew there was no point in arguing. The coach never really listened to any of his players. His own point of view was the only one that mattered to him.

Look, I know you've got loads of skills. And I know being a bit short-sighted doesn't affect your game.

You've got an eye for a goal chance, you can beat defenders on a penny piece, you can pass the ball like a plate.

For the rest of the day Scott's family couldn't get another word out of him. All he could think about was Jed Royce's remarks and wonder whether he would soon be out of the team. Altcar Aces was the best thing in his life. If he didn't play for them he was sure life for him would be terrible.

15

Chapter Two

Scott wanted to say yes, he was hurting badly. Instead, he shook his head.

17

Told you my dad's fitness club was opening soon, didn't I?

U-hum.

Well, next week, but he says we can go and see it tonight, just the two of us. We can try out any of the equipment we like. So, how about that?

It didn't take Scott more than a second to answer.

Hey, sounds good, Ali. Thanks. I'd really like that.

As they fixed the details Scott knew he meant what he said. Ali's father had just retired as a boxer and running the fitness centre was his new career. Scott had never been inside one so he was keen to see what it was like.

The moment he'd finished his tea Scott was on his bike, heading for Ali's home.

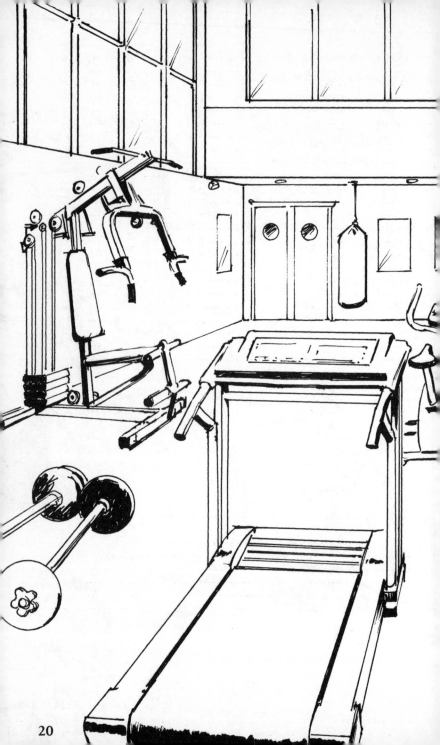

21

Around the walls were posters advertising the fights that Harri Hosein had fought. He'd been a champion at his weight.

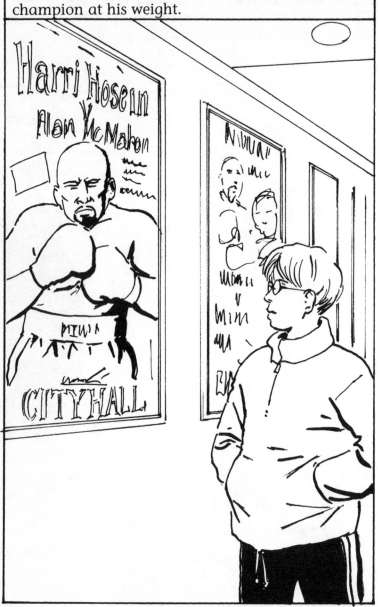

One in particular caught Scott's attention.

A voice breathed in his ear.

Like the idea of boxing, do you, Scott?

He'd never heard a sound as Mr Hosein glided towards him.

Well, maybe.

I'd like to be called Stonefist, though.

Didn't you have a nickname? You know, like Hurricane or Hotfoot?

Oh no, that would mean you would be running away!

I never did that, son! No, but some of the boxing writers said I was hard-hitting. I liked that. I tell you, nobody hit harder than I did. That's important, the harder you hit, the less chance your opponent has of staying with you.

Scott blinked. This was the second bit of advice he'd been given in a few hours about the value of quick hitting.

Why don't you have a go, see how good you are?

Harri demonstrated how to punch with rapid blows, skipping lightly on his toes as he did so.

Let's get you some gloves. Got to do this properly. Ali's already got his own pair but we've got some that'll fit you.

It felt strange to have his hands taped and put on the gloves.

Yeah, that'll do!

Scott was eager to start punching. But...

It's like hitting a concrete wall. I can't move it at all! I must be as weak as a kitten.

Look, son, you've got to put your whole body into it, you've got to use your shoulders.

That's where the power comes from. Go on, use it!

It slowly began to get easier.

Hey!
It moved!
It moved!

All the same, Scott soon felt he'd never done anything so tiring in his life. So he was glad when it was Ali's turn to punch. Of course, his friend had done it before and Scott was impressed by the speed of his punches.

Ali could also manage to blitz the same area, whereas Scott's punches had landed all over the place.

Scott had found his second spell of punching just as tough as the first, but he wasn't going to admit it.

Then, a few minutes later, they were all speeding back home in the sports car. Scott was aching in muscles he'd never known he possessed, but he still felt he'd achieved something at the fitness centre.

Chapter Three

It was training night.

After Kel had finished in a slightly faster time he came over to Scott.

He couldn't believe that Ali had been talking to Kel. He didn't think they knew each other; and Ali wasn't a footballer.

It turned out to be a game of head tennis.
Although he was one of the shorter players Scott had
a good spring in his legs and so could rise higher
than many of the others.

In spite of his height advantage Kel wasn't very accurate with his headers.

On one occasion he missed the ball altogether to the derision of Scott and the others.

They didn't have a practice game and so Scott wasn't able to show the coach how fast he could react to events on the pitch. He was worried that Jed would drop him before he had a chance to prove that he could score whenever he was in sight of goal.

35

They arranged that Scott should visit Kel's home the following Saturday morning.

> He'll be at his fiercest. He seems to know it's the weekend and he can do what he wants – like eat a few people!

> Don't worry, I'll be there. He won't even growl at me.

Scott had always got on well with animals and never felt afraid of them. Somehow they seemed to sense he cared for them.

As a small boy he'd decided he wanted to be a vet and hadn't changed his mind. After all, he could still play football in his spare time. However, he knew how savage a Rottweiler could be. So he took some food titbits with him just in case.

Chapter Four

When he arrived it was Kel's mum who answered the door.

Hello, Mrs Kellerman. I've come to see the dog.

I wouldn't if I were you.

It's a crazy animal. You want to keep well clear of it. You heed my warning, Scott.

For the first time he felt a little nervous. If Kel's mum worried about the Rottweiler then it might be wilder than he'd imagined.

Kel, though, was rubbing his hands with delight.

He's got a compound at the bottom of the garden.

You're in for a treat. Hope you're ready for it!

The frenzied barking started the moment the animal realised a stranger was present. Kel was already talking to it as they approached the wire but that made no difference to the dog's excitement.

Down boy!

What d'you call it, Kel?

Billy.

Indeed, Billy's frantic barking had stopped altogether. There weren't any growls and the hair of his coat was flat. All his aggression seemed to have vanished. He looked as if he were listening to their conversation.

Kel kept blinking as if he couldn't believe what was happening.

Scott didn't bother to reply to that nonsense.

45

Scott announced he had to go.

Listen, I'm really grateful. If there's anything I can do for you, I will.

But I'm still going to finish the season as the Aces' top-scorer. I won't let you take that away from me, Scott.

Oh, we'll see about that.

Chapter Five

When Scott came off the treadmill at the Fitness Centre Ali was waiting for him.

Scott wanted to be on top form for Altcar Aces' away game at Weather Hill, one of the League's poorer teams. Scott saw it as an opportunity to increase his goal tally and perhaps catch up on Kel's total. Kel himself was doubtful because he'd hurt his ankle during training. Jed Royce had lined up a replacement, called Warren, who'd never played a full match for them so far; he'd merely come on as a sub on a couple of occasions.

Scott got changed. He was feeling good about the game. He'd been training hard on his own and thought his form had come back. His new fitness routine was perhaps paying off.

Then, just as Jed Royce was beginning his last-minute team talk, Kel burst in.

Sorry I'm late, boss. Had to go to the chemist's for my mum's medicine.

With an explanation like that the coach couldn't blame his leading striker for his lateness.

Just get changed, quick as you can, son. Warren, you'll be on the bench now.

Warren didn't look too unhappy.

Hey, those tablets for Billy are fantastic. He's like a new dog. Fiercer than ever. You did a great job, mate. I owe you one. I brought Billy to the match. A mate of mine's minding him.

Scott smiled. He was glad to hear about Billy's health but disappointed that Kel would have a chance to add to his goal tally after all. What's more, his co-striker was plainly in the best of moods.

Weather Hill didn't begin like a weak side. They were fast, eager, physical. Scott was clattered the first time he had the ball.

The downpour was making the pitch very
slippery but Scott could cope with that. His
speed and bewildering changes of direction left
many opponents in despair.
One of his passes put
Kel through.

But Kel blazed the ball wildly over the bar.

Scott had the impression that Kel wasn't really fit enough to be playing. When his tall team-mate went down under another brutal tackle he needed lengthy treatment from Jed before he could hobble back into the game.

Then Kel was fouled on the edge of the box. The free kick was taken quickly and for once the Weather Hill defence was caught napping.

Kel was free. He rounded the goalkeeper...

...and an open goal lay before him.

But instead of putting the ball in the net he slipped it sideways.

Scott was so surprised he almost miskicked. Luckily, though, he recovered. A second later the net bulged.

That's the one I owed you, just don't expect another!

So the Aces won 1-0 to keep up their promotion challenge. If they hadn't, Jed told Kel, he'd never have forgiven him. Kel wasn't really listening. His ankle injury had flared up again.

Well played, Scott.

You're doing all the right things at last. But you nearly missed that sitter. Don't do it again. Hit 'em, remember!

Scott nodded and went home to practise his kicking.

Chapter Six

When, three weeks later, it was the last match of the season, the Aces needed just one point for promotion; and Kel was their top-scorer, one goal ahead of Scott.

Kel still hadn't really got over his ankle injury and had missed two games. Scott, his confidence increasing match by match, believed he could yet snatch the trophy for the team's best marksman.

Look, what we need here is an early goal and then we can sit on our lead for the rest of the game, make sure we get at least a draw out of it.

As usual, defence dominated Jed's thinking.

Kel was testing the strapping on his ankle.

If I can get six goals, I will. One goal's never enough.

Dodlee, their opponents, were a mid-table side with little to play for but they still fancied finishing the season on a winning note. So they started with a rush and pinned the Aces in their own half.

Twice they almost got the ball in the net because of a jittery defence.

Jed was getting redder in the face by the second.

Scott got the benefit when defence did clear the ball and he picked it up in midfield. For, as he ran at them, one opponent slipped on the soft ground and another mis-timed his tackle completely.

...and Kel converted it.

Ali, on the touchline as a supporter, cheered madly.

It was hard to tell who was the more ecstatic, Jed or Kel. Scott was happy for both of them but knew now he had no real chance of taking the goal-scoring award, even though minutes later Kel limped off after another fierce knock on his ankle. Jed reorganised the team defensively and Scott was ordered to stay back.

With their defence able to move up to join their attack, Dodlee gradually got back into the game. Scott was getting through a lot of work but not enjoying it. His game was all about getting forward, and that wasn't allowed...

...not even when, in the
second half, Dodlee equalised.

The Aces had the point they needed but might not hang on to it because Dodlee were attacking ceaselessly.

Then someone miskicked badly, the ball ballooned into the air before spinning backwards towards the Dodlee goal.

Scott was the only player who might reach it.

Go for it Scott, you'll get it!

Scott raced towards the box.

He was almost there when a tackle from
behind brought him down.

Dodlee hurriedly formed a defensive wall. But the Aces players were in no hurry.

Scott had other ideas.

This is mine!

He placed the ball and looked at the wall that had formed in front of him.

He could see a gap and he was going to make the most of his hours of shooting practice.

He was going to hit it as hard as he'd ever hit any ball in his life.

It went through the chosen space like a rocket. The Dodlee goalie didn't even see it as it went past him and lifted the net.

It was the goal that clinched promotion.

The ref blew for time almost immediately.

Oh wonderful, great strike! You really hit that one, Scott.

My best goal ever.

Until the next one!